Cha

S0-ADP-162

...nder School Library

Chandler School Library

E.C.I.A., Chapter 2
P.L. 97-35

Mystery at the Ball Game

Chandler School Library

Mystery at the Ball Game

BY R. PARKER McVEY

Illustrations by Jackie Rogers

FIC MCV
2-02
1304083

Library of Congress Cataloging in Publication Data

McVey, R. Parker.
    Mystery at the ball game.

    (Solve-it-yourself)
    Summary: The reader, overhearing a conversation about
a plot to kidnap a millionaire's son at a Little League
game, makes decisions which determine the outcome of the
story.
    1. Plot-your-own stories. 2. Children's stories,
American. [1. Plot-your-own stories. 2. Mystery and
detective stories. 3. Kidnapping—Fiction. 4. Baseball
—Fiction] I. Rogers, Jackie, ill. II. Title. III. Series.
PZ7.M47884My   1985   [Fic]   84-8486
ISBN 0-8167-0336-1 (lib. bdg.)
ISBN 0-8167-0337-X (pbk.)

Copyright © 1985 by Troll Associates, Mahwah, New Jersey
All rights reserved. No part of this book may be used or
reproduced in any manner whatsoever without written
permission from the publisher.
Printed in the United States of America.

10   9   8   7   6   5   4   3   2   1

Warning!

In this story, *you* are the detective! *You* must find the clues, follow the leads, and try to solve the mystery.

But do not read this book from beginning to end. Start on page 1, and keep reading till you come to a choice. After that, the story is up to you. Your decisions will take you from page to page.

Think carefully before you decide. Some choices will lead you to further clues. But other choices may bring about a quick end to your investigation—and to you!

Whatever happens, you can always go back to the beginning and start again. Best of luck in your investigation.

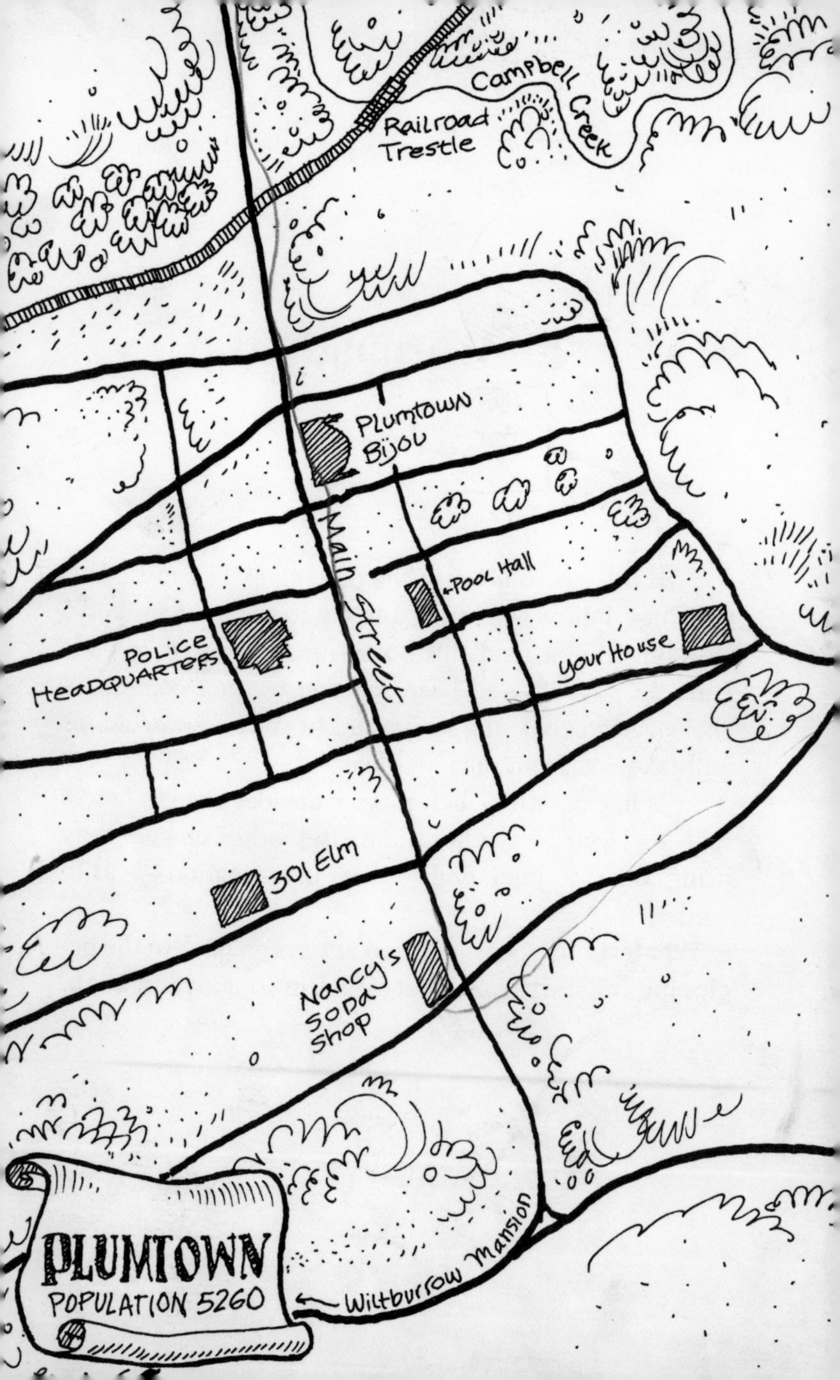

Campbell Creek
Railroad Trestle
Plumtown Bijou
Main Street
Pool Hall
Police Headquarters
your House
301 Elm
Nancy's Soda Shop
Wiltburrow Mansion
PLUMTOWN
POPULATION 5260

Shed

House

Short Cut

Bleachers

Parking Lot

Mrs. Puddington's

STRETCH

YOU

JIMMY "IQ" PETERS

MRS. PRISCILLA
ODDINGTON

JAST
PEE

BRONCO
BLACKBURNE

MARTIN BROADAXE

CAPPY
WILTBURROW

MR. FREDERICK G. WILTBURROW

WALDORF

It is close to eleven o'clock at night, prime time for stargazing. Your good friend, Jimmy "IQ" Peters, has persuaded you to go with him to the Plumtown baseball diamond. IQ is eager for you to try out his new telescope.

When you arrive at the field, IQ sets up the telescope near second base. The stars are brilliant tonight. There is no moon and not a cloud in the sky.

IQ offers you the first look through the telescope. You put your eye to the viewer. Immediately, you recognize the Andromeda galaxy.

"Wow," you say.

"Rather spectacular, isn't it, old friend?" IQ says.

After a few minutes, you turn the telescope over to IQ. Well-known at school for his nimble intelligence, your friend slowly sweeps his new instrument across the sky.

As IQ becomes more absorbed in the heavens, you notice that the night air seems particularly fresh. Taking a deep breath, you realize that you feel better now than you've felt all day. IQ, you can see, is lost in some far galaxy. Not wanting to bother him, you stroll toward the outfield.

When you reach dead center, you stop for a moment, remembering with pride the awesome home run you belted right over this very spot just last week. It was great to hear the crowd and your teammates cheer as you rounded the bases. That homer won the game, and it made your name as a ballplayer.

Now you are doubly famous. You are already Plumtown's most respected amateur detective. Ever since you hunted down the missing dog of Mrs. Priscilla Puddington, a local heiress, you have worked on many important cases. Sergeant Stretch of the Plumtown Police Department has now begun to call you in on some of his investigations.

As you lean against the outfield fence and look up dreamily at the sky, a rustling sound in the thick woods beyond the fence disturbs you. Twigs break. The sounds seem to be coming from about fifty feet away.

You feel a sudden chill. Footsteps are moving in your direction. The steps are slow and sinister, and by listening carefully you figure out that there are two people. You crouch down behind the fence and carefully peek over the top of it.

In the dim starlight, you barely see the outline of two men in the woods. They have stopped walking, and now stand less than twenty feet away.

"The kid always takes this path after a game," one of the men says in a low, deep voice.

"Does he ride a bicycle?" asks the other.

"Are you kidding? He walks to the other side of the woods, where the chauffeur picks him up. He doesn't like the other kids to see him get into such a big car."

"Right. So we grab him somewhere around the bend in the path back there."

The speaker pauses as the other man lights a cigar. In the flicker of light from the match, you see an outline of the man's face. But before you have a chance to study his features, and before he has a chance to finish what he is saying, IQ yells out to you—something about how great Mars looks.

Instantly the man puts out the match. Then both men turn and walk away into the woods. Trying to hold onto the image of the face that you saw so briefly, you race back to the infield.

"IQ," you whisper, "you won't believe what I just heard."

"From where you were standing, I'd guess it was a conversation between two young bullfrogs."

"No, IQ," you say. "Two men in the woods beyond center field were talking about grabbing some kid."

"What!"
You quickly tell IQ what you saw and heard.
"It's a kidnapping in the works!" he exclaims.
"Exactly!"
"We have to do something," says IQ.

If you think it would be best to work with the police on this case, turn to page 8.

If you decide to begin the investigation on your own, turn to page 11.

If you decide to wait for tomorrow night's game and see what happens, turn to page 15.

6

Stretch plunges into the woods like a silent tiger, with you and IQ right behind.

Through the trees, IQ spots the bobbing head of the young Wiltburrow heir moving along the far end of the path. Stretch also sees him now, but there is no sign of the kidnappers. Stretch slows down and stops.

"I think we should just get hold of the kid and protect him," Stretch says. "We can flush out the kidnappers later."

You and IQ look at one another, wondering whether or not that is the right way to handle the situation. But there is no time for second-guessing.

Stretch hurries toward the path to intercept Cappy.

Suddenly an ominous figure rises up from behind a boulder that Stretch has just passed. Before you can shout a warning, the large figure strikes the back of Stretch's head.

You and IQ freeze in your tracks. Things happen so quickly, you barely have time to move. You watch, speechless, as a second man pounces on Cappy Wiltburrow. At the same moment, the menacing brute who stopped Stretch turns and charges you and IQ.

You both turn to run, but your legs are like jelly. You feel yourself swept forward, face down, onto the ground. Then there is darkness.

THE END

You wait for Big Martin Broadaxe to walk away from the shed. Then you pick up a large stone from the ground and use it to try to break open the padlock on the shed door.

With one hard smash the lock opens for you. You look inside the shed and see IQ's feet sticking out from behind a rolled-up plastic tarp. You go over and get down on your knees so that you can untie him.

Suddenly, the light from the door is blocked. You turn quickly to see the ominous outline of Big Martin standing in the doorway.

He comes into the shed and takes a swipe at you with his huge hand. You dodge him and make a lunge for the door.

You are just about through the door when Broadaxe grabs your shirt from behind and jerks you back inside. In the distance, the last thing you see before the big groundskeeper swings the door to the shed closed is Stretch's car pulling into the parking lot. Your only hope is that Stretch will search the area until he finds you.

THE END

8

from page 5

First thing next morning, you and IQ go to the Plumtown police headquarters. Sergeant Stretch, who likes you and admires your detective work, listens carefully to your story.

"You're absolutely right," he says. "You tapped into a kidnapping plot. Any ideas who the victim might be?"

"Well," you say, "IQ and I have decided, through a process of elimination, that it's probably Cappy Wiltburrow. His father owns a shipbuilding company, and Cappy plays on a baseball team. *And*, both IQ and I have seen him leave games by the path through the woods."

"Sounds right," Stretch says. "Any ideas about who the kidnappers might be?"

"No ideas, just impressions," you say. "The man who lit the match appeared to be big. His head was also large. And something about the other man's voice was familiar to me."

"Can you associate the voice with a place?" asks IQ.

"I don't know," you say.

"How about other sounds and smells?" IQ asks. "Does that voice remind you of music, or the sound of a railroad, or the smell of burgers frying, or..."

"Wait," you say. "Yes, I think I heard that voice at the movie theater a few nights ago. I associate it with the smell of popcorn."

Stretch interrupts, "Can you picture a face?"

"No, the voice at the theater was behind me, but I remember that it was a man complaining to someone about the price of his ticket. He had a kind of whining voice."

"Anything else?" asks Stretch with excitement.

"No," you say, "the rest is a blank. But at least we can see that he's someone who might have been around town before."

IQ looks up at the clock on the wall.

"It's ten o'clock," he says. "We should get moving."

Stretch turns to you. "Where do you think we should go from here?" he asks.

If you decide to go directly to Wiltburrow Manor and talk with Cappy's father, turn to page 20.

If you decide to go to the Plumtown movie theater to dig up a lead on the man whose voice you heard, turn to page 79.

from page 5

You get up early the next morning and begin your own investigation. The first thing you do is put in a call to Mrs. Priscilla Puddington, eccentric Plumtown heiress. Mrs. Puddington knows almost all there is to know about everyone in Plumtown.

She has been a good friend and ally of yours ever since you helped recover her missing Lhaso apso. The dog had been stolen by a couple of local roughnecks, who planned to sell it for a good price in another town.

"Good morning, my dear young friend," she says when she hears your voice over the phone.

"Good morning, Mrs. Puddington," you say. "Could I stop by to see you this morning? There is a grave matter that I would like to discuss with you."

"A grave matter?" says Mrs. Puddington. "I shall be delighted to discuss a grave matter with you. Come right over. And bring that charming friend of yours along."

As you hang up the phone, you turn to IQ: "She wants you to come, too."

You and IQ hop onto your bicycles and pedal to the outskirts of town to Mrs. Puddington's large, stately house.

When you knock on the door, the heiress greets you herself. She leads you into her library, where she spends much of her time.

"Now," she says as you all sit down, "what is this grave matter?"

You tell her what you heard last night. She listens carefully and nods her head, holding a finger to her lips.

"Well," she says, "we do know who the victim will be, don't we?"

"Yes, we do," you say.

"It will be Cappy Wiltburrow," IQ says with great certainty. "He is the only kid in town who would be picked up by a limousine after a game. And both of us have seen him leave the ball field by that path through the woods."

"Indeed," Mrs. Puddington says. "Little Cappy is the son of my old rival, Frederick G. Wiltburrow. Cappy is the only boy in town those men could have been talking about."

"Do you have any idea who could be behind this plot?" you ask.

You watch as Mrs. Puddington's eyes dart up toward the ceiling. She is checking the extensive records of many Plumtown residents—their characters, and their comings and goings—that she keeps inside her head.

After almost a minute, Mrs. Puddington clears her throat and speaks.

"There are four people who come to mind. Each has either a bad reputation or other disturbing qualities that lead me to suspect that they would be party to such a plot."

"Could you give me those names?" you ask as you take out your pad and pencil.

"First," she says, "there's that awful Mr. Jastrow Peevler. Watch out for him. He's a dangerous little snake."

"Do you know his whereabouts?" IQ asks.

"Yes, and you know his house, too. It's the one on Elm Street that looks as though it is abandoned. That's not abandonment, though. That is *neglect*," Mrs. Puddington notes with disgust.

"We do know that house," you say. "Who are the others that you suspect?"

"Well," she says, "there is that big fellow who tends the ball field, Martin Broadaxe. He's a shifty-eyed sort and might be involved, though he certainly wouldn't be the mastermind.

"Then," she says, "you must consider that wretched fellow about whom I've learned so little, Bronco Blackburne. He fits your description of a man with a large head.

"Finally," says Mrs. Puddington, "one must always keep one's eye out for the long shot. My father taught me that. And the long shot I'm thinking of is dear old Waldorf, the butler to the Wiltburrow family. *That* fellow has *always* bothered me."

"We'd better get right on top of these leads," you say, turning to IQ.

"We've got a lot to do before tonight's game," IQ says.

"I want you both to be very careful, and to keep me informed by phone," Mrs. Puddington says, getting up to show you out.

You both thank Mrs. Puddington for her help, and head out to your bicycles.

Turn to page 24.

You decide to go to the game and keep your eyes open for trouble.

In the bottom of the third inning, your team, the Cowboys, trails the Braves by a run, seven to six.

The Cowboys are the home team, so they are coming up to bat. You will hit fourth this inning.

As the pitcher for the Braves takes his warm-up throws, you look out to center field. There you see Cappy Wiltburrow, center fielder for the Braves.

Doubt creeps into your mind. Should you have warned him, or gone to Sergeant Stretch, or even pursued an investigation of your own? You are certain of one thing: there is nothing worse than setting off a false alarm.

What did you really hear last night? Can you trust your deduction that a kidnapping plot is under way, and that Cappy Wiltburrow is the victim?

You have taken a wait-and-see attitude. IQ is sitting in the bleachers behind home plate, watching the woods beyond center field with his binoculars. You have looked up at him several times for a signal that something unusual is going on. So far he has seen nothing out of the ordinary.

You know Sergeant Stretch's telephone number and are prepared to alert him if you sense that trouble is brewing. Meanwhile, you must try to concentrate on helping your team catch up.

The first batter for the Cowboys bunts the ball right down the third-base line. The bunt takes the third baseman by surprise, and he lets it roll, hoping it will go foul.

The ball stays fair. It rolls right down the line and hits the bag at third, a perfect bunt. That puts the tying run on first base.

The next batter jumps on the first pitch and hits a nasty drive to deep right-center field. Cappy Wilt-burrow gets an excellent jump on the ball and makes a fine backhanded catch against the fence. He turns and fires the ball back to the infield. Now there is one out.

Cappy, you can see, has an excellent arm. You will remember to be careful about trying to take an extra base on anything hit out to him.

Now you are on deck. Billy Kroger, your team's catcher, is at the plate. Billy swings at the first pitch and chops it into the dirt in front of the plate. The ball takes a high bounce toward the pitcher, who waits for it to come down. He catches the ball easily, then fires it to first. Billy really hustles down the line, but he's out by a step. Meanwhile, the runner on first moves over to second.

With two down, you step up to the plate. Your mind has hardly been on the game, but now the chips are down. Your team trails by a run and there is a runner in scoring position. It's your job to drive him in. You dig in at the plate and bear down.

When the count reaches one ball, two strikes, you step out of the batter's box to think the situation over. You have faced this pitcher before. You know that when he is ahead on the count he doesn't like to give the batter anything good to hit. So you've got to be careful not to go after a bad pitch.

The next pitch is a slider, low and away. The count stands at two and two.

The pitcher, you believe, does not want to waste another pitch. You think that he'll come back with a hard fastball. And he does.

Your swing is even and quick, and you line the ball to the right of second base, just over the outstretched glove of the diving second baseman. The runner on second heads for home as the ball rolls into the gap in right-center field.

As you round the bag at first, you see that Cappy Wiltburrow is just about to field the ball. Your split-second decision is to try for a double, in spite of Cappy's powerful arm. You put your head down and give it all you've got.

You see the shortstop position himself to take the ball and slap on the tag. You lunge forward in a perfect head-first slide. But Cappy's throw is perfect too, and you are out. That ends the inning, but you have driven in the tying run.

Turn to page 27.

from page 10

You, IQ, and Stretch drive out to Wiltburrow Manor, a stately mansion hidden from public view by dense woods. The three of you are greeted at the front door by Waldorf, butler to the Wiltburrow family.

"We'd like to speak with Mr. Wiltburrow," Stretch says.

"May I tell him who is calling?" Waldorf looks the three of you up and down.

"Sergeant Stretch of the Plumtown police, and friends," Stretch says as he holds out his police shield and identification.

"Of course, sir. Won't you please be seated in here?" Waldorf says, leading you into a large oak-paneled sitting room. "I'll tell Mr. Wiltburrow you are here."

The three of you have barely settled into comfortable leather chairs when Frederick G. Wiltburrow enters the room.

After you introduce yourselves, Mr. Wiltburrow turns to Sergeant Stretch and asks, "What can I do for you, Sergeant?"

"Sorry to have to tell you this, sir, but we have good reason to believe that we have uncovered a plot to kidnap your son, Casper," says Stretch.

"What!" exclaims Mr. Wiltburrow.

Stretch tells the whole story. For a moment Mr. Wiltburrow is speechless.

Finally he says, "Cappy is out hiking with a friend. I don't expect him back until late this afternoon. Is he in immediate danger?"

"No, we don't think so," Stretch says. "It looks like the kidnappers plan to grab him after his ball game tonight. I fully intend to protect your son, but I want to catch the criminals as well."

As Stretch continues to speak with Mr. Wiltburrow, you notice the shadow of someone standing outside the doorway. You begin to get up to see who is out there, but IQ puts his hand on your shoulder to restrain you.

"It's better to let him think we don't know he's there," IQ whispers.

"You're right," you whisper back.

Stretch continues to question Mr. Wiltburrow. Both of them are unaware that someone else is listening.

"Have you noticed anything strange lately, anything out of the ordinary?" Stretch asks.

"Come to think of it," Mr. Wiltburrow says, "on two occasions when I've been out with Cappy, I've noticed a heavyset man staring at us. When I looked directly back at him, his reaction was most disturbing. Both times he turned quickly and hurried away. The experience left me a bit nervous, but I thought no more of it until now."

Stretch gets up and thanks Mr. Wiltburrow, while trying to reassure him about Cappy's safety. Then the three of you go back outside to the car.

Stretch turns to you. "The heavyset man seen by Mr. Wiltburrow sounds like the guy you saw behind the baseball diamond."

"It sure does," you say. "We'd better find that man, and fast."

Then IQ reminds you that someone was just listening in on the conversation the three of you were having with Mr. Wiltburrow.

"Any suggestions?" Stretch asks.

"Maybe the butler is involved," IQ suggests.

If you decide to visit the Plumtown Billiard Hall to talk to your contacts there, turn to page 31.

If you tell Stretch and IQ to wait for you just beyond the gates of Wiltburrow Manor while you look for a way to get back inside the mansion, turn to page 99.

from page 14

You and IQ pedal your bicycles furiously back to town. As you pull up even with him you say, "Let's check out the groundskeeper first."

"What's your reasoning?"

"He's the easiest to get to—he's right at the ball field. And from Mrs. Puddington's description, he sounds like the weakest of the bunch. We might be able to trick him into revealing something."

"If," IQ says, "he knows anything to begin with."

"Right," you say.

As you ride into town, you signal a right-hand turn at the short cut to the baseball diamond. You arrive at the field in less than two minutes.

As you walk through the gate by first base and onto the field, you see Big Martin Broadaxe, the groundskeeper, raking the dirt out by third base. His back is to you and you startle him when you say hello.

It strikes you as funny that you have never really noticed him before. He always seemed so quiet and out of the way. But now, for the first time, you see the shifty-eyed expression that Mrs. Puddington mentioned.

"Could we talk to you?" IQ asks.

"About what?"

"We were just wondering," you say, "if you have seen Mr. Jastrow Peevler or Mr. Bronco Blackburne? My friend and I were supposed to meet them here today."

Big Martin Broadaxe looks at you, then at IQ, then back at you. He looks mistrustful of you, but, then again, you guess that he probably mistrusts everyone.

"I don't know either of those guys," he says, and then turns his back on you and resumes raking the dirt.

"Well," you say, "we were going to discuss Cappy Wiltburrow with them."

At the mention of Cappy's name, Big Martin stops raking the dirt. There is a long pause.

"That's the little rich kid," he says, turning again in your direction.

"Yes," IQ says, "his family is very wealthy."

"Yeah," Big Martin says with a strange smile, "very wealthy. "

"What else do you know about Cappy Wiltburrow?" you ask.

"Nothing," he says. "Now leave me alone. I've got work to do."

With your head you motion to IQ, and the two of you walk away. You leave the field.

"What do you think?" you ask when both of you are behind the dugout with your bicycles.

"I don't know," IQ says, "but he certainly bears watching."

"Do you want to handle that?"

"It would be a pleasure," IQ says. "Let's ride out of here and then I'll double back. I'll find a spot where I can keep an eye on him. What are you going to do?"

"Well," you say, "we still have to consider Peevler, Blackburne, and Waldorf."

You get on your bicycle and ride away, with IQ right behind you. When you're a few hundred yards away from the field, IQ tips his cap, turns around, and heads back.

"Be careful," you say to your best friend as you part company.

"Don't worry about me," IQ says with a wink and a smile.

Now you are alone, and you have decisions to make. First you decide to hold off on approaching Waldorf, the Wiltburrow butler.

If you decide to check out Jastrow Peevler, turn to page 88.

If you decide to investigate Bronco Blackburne, turn to page 33.

The score of the game remains tied at seven-all through the fifth inning.

Before you trot out to your position in center field for the top of the sixth and last inning, you again look up to the bleachers for a sign from IQ. He shrugs his shoulders to indicate that he sees nothing. Both the game and the plot to kidnap Cappy Wiltburrow are going down to the wire.

As the Braves come to bat for the top of the sixth inning, you try as hard as you can to concentrate on the game.

The first batter for the Braves slaps a line drive just inside the foul pole in right field for an easy double. From the center field you watch Billy Kroger, your catcher, walk out to the mound. He is probably trying to get your pitcher, Keith White, to settle down.

Billy Kroger's efforts succeed. Keith strikes out the next two hitters. Now he needs only one more out to set the Braves down. Up to the plate steps Cappy Wiltburrow.

Cappy is known around the league as a tough out. He rarely is struck out. He usually gets a hit, and he is able to hit the ball to all fields. You position yourself moderately deep and straightaway in center.

After the count reaches two and two, Cappy strokes a solid single right up the middle. You charge the ball, and fire it to the plate to catch the runner attempting to score from second. Your throw is half a second late, and the Braves lead eight to seven.

The next batter pops up for the third out. The Cowboys will come to bat in the bottom of the sixth, down by a run.

The first batter for the Cowboys strikes out on three pitches. Billy Kroger, the next batter, crowds the plate and is hit in the leg by a pitch. He trots down to first. There is now one out and one man on base.

You step up to the plate. You must face the same pitcher you faced three innings earlier, and you can see that he is still bothered by your previous hit. You know that you hit his best pitch. You wonder if he will pitch around you—give you little, if anything, to hit. He might let you walk unless you go after bad pitches. But that would mean he'd be putting the winning run on base. You figure that's not his style.

He's going to come at you with his fastball. You can see that from the way he is working himself up out on the mound.

The first pitch sizzles past you, chin high, for a ball. Watch out, you think, this guy is giving it all he's got. The second pitch arrives, down the middle. You swing late and foul it into the backstop.

You take the opportunity to turn around and glance up at IQ in the bleachers. You can see that he has his binoculars trained on the woods beyond the center-field fence.

The next pitch is down the middle, but so fast that you can't even swing at it. It's a strike. Now the count is one ball, two strikes. You must concentrate.

Once again, the pitcher rears back and fires. But this time you are ready. You swing, and connect with great force. The ball rises high and deep toward center field. Cappy Wiltburrow goes back, back, back to the fence. He makes a tremendous leaping try for the ball. But it's gone—a home run!

As you round first base, you go into your home run trot. You have won another game for your team. As you reach second base you can see that Cappy Wiltburrow is leaning against the fence where your ball went out. His head hangs down in disappointment.

The wild cheers of your teammates and the crowd seem almost far away from you. You've done your job for the team. Now it's Cappy Wiltburrow's safety that concerns you. As you round third base, you look back over your shoulder to see that Cappy is in the process of hopping over the center-field fence.

"Oh, no!" you say to yourself. "He's about to leave. He's going straight to the path."

The instant that your foot comes down on home plate with the winning run, you are mobbed by your teammates. But as you gratefully accept their congratulations, you are already pulling away. You must move quickly. You look up toward the bleachers. IQ has disappeared!

If you race from the field and then out toward the woods after Cappy Wiltburrow, turn to page 35.

If you are worried about IQ, and feel you must try to find him, turn to page 93.

from page 23

Pulling up to the Plumtown Billiard Hall, you say to Stretch and IQ, "Let me handle this alone. These guys get nervous talking to the police, and I already know a couple of them from other cases."

While Stretch and IQ wait outside, you enter the hall.

"Hi, kid," says old Bob Brown, the manager.

"How are you, Bob? Is 'the Ear' around?" you ask.

"He's in the back room."

You walk through the doorway into the back room, where you find Jimmy "the Ear" chalking the tip of his pool stick. A few other players are waiting their turns.

You motion the Ear off to the side. He joins you near a vending machine. As you put some coins into the machine, you describe the heavily built man you are looking for.

"Sounds like Blackburne," says the Ear. "He's a real mystery man. He started showing up around town a month or two ago. Lousy pool shooter. Nobody knows anything about him. Calls himself Bronco."

"Where could I find him right now?" you ask.

"Can't say for sure," says the Ear, "but he talks a lot about ice cream. You might find him at Nancy's Soda Shop. That's the best I can do, kid."

"That's swell, Ear. Thanks for your help."

You rejoin Stretch and IQ outside and give them the information. All three of you hop into Stretch's car and head across town to Nancy's.

"Do you think we'll have time for a quick banana split?" IQ asks.

"Only if the man we're looking for is there, IQ," you say.

Stretch parks his car around the corner from Nancy's, and the three of you get out and walk toward the front entrance of the soda shop. When you are about ten yards from the entrance, out walks Waldorf, the Wiltburrow butler. Without seeing you, he turns and walks up the street in the opposite direction.

"I think something fishy is going on here," IQ says, remembering the shadow that you both saw in the doorway at Wiltburrow Manor.

You have to make a split-second decision.

If you tell Stretch and IQ to go into Nancy's, then follow Waldorf on your own, turn to page 120.

If you go into Nancy's to see if you can meet Bronco Blackburne, turn to page 37.

from page 26

Mrs. Puddington admitted to you that she knew all too little about Bronco Blackburne. But if there is any information at all on him, your contact at the Plumtown Billiard Hall, the Ear, should have it.

You pedal down Main Street to the billiard hall. You lean your bicycle against a traffic sign out front and walk in.

"Hi, kid," says Bob Brown, the owner.

"Hi, Bob. Is 'the Ear' on the premises?" you ask.

"Yeah, kid, in the back room."

You stroll casually through the doorway to the back room. You spot the Ear sitting by himself in a dark corner. He sees you approach.

"Sit down kid," the Ear says. "You look worried."

"I need some information," you say.

"Anything I have is yours. You've always been good to me."

"What can you tell me about Bronco Blackburne?" you ask.

A dark expression comes over the Ear's face. If you had to guess, you would say that he was afraid.

"Blackburne's a bad one. You have to watch your back with him."

"What can you tell me?" you ask.

"Two things," he says. "One, he's involved with somebody who is very powerful. And, two, at this time of day you'll find him at Nancy's Soda Shop. Black-burne eats more ice cream than any man alive."

"That's all?" you ask.

"That's it, kid."

"Thanks, Ear," you say as you turn to leave. Now you must decide what to do next.

If you choose to confront Blackburne yourself, turn to page 41.

If you want to pick up IQ first so that he can back you up, turn to page 95.

from page 30

As you reach the path that Cappy took into the woods, you realize that serious trouble may well lie ahead. You slow down a bit and proceed with more caution.

When you reach a bend in the path, you stop. Cautiously, you peek around the side of a fat tree. But you see nothing. No Cappy. No kidnappers.

You walk slowly along the path until you come to a spot that shows signs of a struggle. But you can't tell much more than that.

You decide to take the path all the way out to the road. If the Wiltburrow limousine is not there, you can assume that Cappy made it safely through the woods and is on his way home.

But, as you follow the path up an embankment and onto the shoulder of the road, you find the limo and chauffeur still waiting for Cappy.

Gifford, the Wiltburrow chauffeur, sees you coming.

"Is the game over?" he asks.

"Yes. Have you seen Cappy?"

"Why, no," he says. "Have you?"

"I saw him take the path and then I followed him, but he disappeared," you say.

"Master Cappy has disappeared!" Gifford says. "My goodness, what should we do?"

"Drive to the nearest phone and call Sergeant Stretch of the Plumtown Police. Tell him to come to the ball field as soon as possible. Explain to him that Cappy is missing and that he may have been kidnapped."

With that you turn and run back into the woods.

If you stop to look for clues on the path where you saw signs of a struggle, turn to page 48.

If you go back to the ball field to look for IQ, turn to page 98.

As Waldorf quickly walks away, the three of you enter Nancy's.

"Blackburne is probably sitting in the last booth," IQ says. He guesses that Blackburne is the kind of man who likes to sit where he can see everything and everyone.

You look toward the back, but see only a couple of kids sharing a banana split in the next-to-last booth.

Stretch turns toward the counter. Nancy, the proprietor, walks over to him.

"Hi, Sarge," Nancy says.

"Hi, Nance," Stretch replies. "That butler fellow who was just in here, did he talk to anyone?"

"Old Waldorf? No," she says. "He just came in and looked around for a minute, then left. He was probably looking for his big friend, but that fellow left an hour ago. He's turning into my best customer— averages about three hot-fudge sundaes a sitting."

"Any idea where the big guy went?" Stretch says.

"Sorry, Sarge, he just comes and goes. He's very touchy, just likes to be left alone."

"Where does he sit?" IQ asks.

"Always sits in that last booth over there," Nancy says.

While Stretch continues to question Nancy, you and IQ walk down to Blackburne's booth.

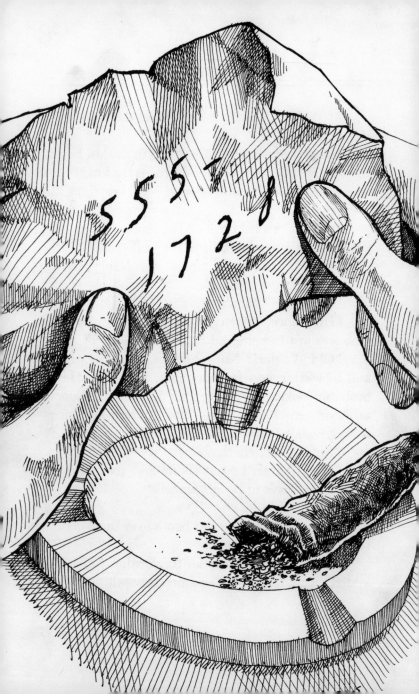

The ashtray contains the butt of a half-smoked cigar and a crumpled-up piece of paper. You smooth out the paper. It's a sales ticket from the Universal Hardware store, just down the street. Written on the back is a telephone number.

Just as you are about to tell IQ what you've found, he pops up from below the table.

"Look at this," he says, holding out a small clump of red mud in the palm of his hand.

Forgetting for a second the sales slip with the telephone number, you take the red mud from IQ and study it.

"There's only one place around Plumtown where you find red mud like this," you say.

"That's right," IQ says. "Out by Campbell Creek under the railroad trestle. Mr. Spivak pointed that out in science class."

"And one other thing, IQ," you say. "There's an old shed under the trestle that the railroad construction crew used when they made repairs."

You both walk over to Stretch, who is now thanking Nancy for her help. You nod to him and head for the door.

Once you get outside, Stretch says, "Nancy really didn't have much more to offer, but it's definitely Blackburne. Did you guys find anything?"

"You bet we did, Sergeant," you say. Then you tell Stretch about the mud and the telephone number. Now you have two excellent leads.

If you decide to trace the number and find out to whom it belongs, turn to page 103.

If you decide to investigate the shed below the railroad trestle, turn to page 45.

from page 34

You ride your bicycle over to Nancy's Soda Shop, which is only a few blocks away from the billiard hall. Before you go inside, you stop and think about what the Ear said of Blackburne. He urged you to "watch your back."

You enter Nancy's and look around. Blackburne, whom you immediately recognize because of his big head, is in the last booth, eating ice cream. You walk directly to the booth.

"Mr. Blackburne?" you inquire.

"Go away!" he says in a voice that sounds like the engine of a cement truck.

But you won't be stopped so easily.

"Does the name Cappy Wiltburrow interest you at all?" you say.

Later you will swear to IQ that you saw steam come out of Blackburne's ears when you mentioned Cappy's name.

"Sit down," he orders.

You take the bench opposite Blackburne. He pushes aside several empty ice-cream dishes and wipes his mouth with a dirty napkin.

"What do you know about Cappy Wiltburrow?" Blackburne asks gruffly.

"I think someone wants to hurt him," you reply.

"Oh, yeah?" the big man says. "And who is that?"

"Maybe someone who wants to get a lot of money from Cappy's father. Maybe you, Mr. Blackburne."

Blackburne reaches across the table and grabs you by the front of your sweatshirt with his enormous hand.

"You're some smart kid, but you haven't learned not to go around accusing law-abiding citizens of bad intentions, especially when you have no proof."

"Well, Mr. Blackburne," you say as you push away his hand, "just show up at the baseball clubhouse before tonight's game. I'll be there with all the proof I need. And if you don't show up, you'll be sorry."

"I'll be there, kid, because I got nothing to worry about. And after you're through, we'll see who'll be sorry."

You get up and walk away. You want Blackburne to guess at what you know and how you found it out.

Your own best guess at this point is that Blackburne is involved, and that it was he you heard in the woods the night before. The size of the head is right and the voice is the same.

But there may be a lot more to the plot to kidnap Cappy Wiltburrow than you had originally thought. If, as the Ear has claimed, Blackburne is working with

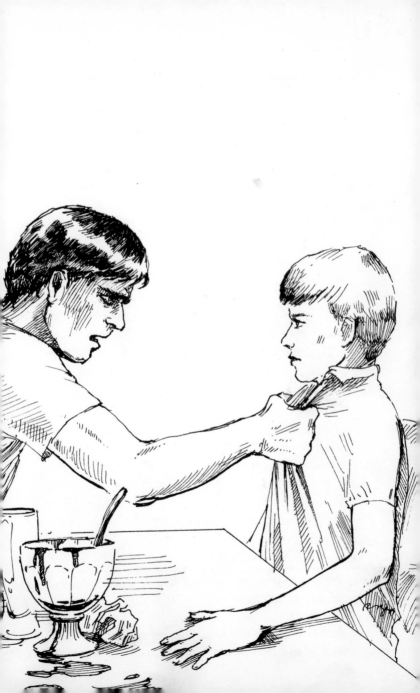

someone powerful, then how could the motive be money?

And if the motive is not money, then what is it?

You decide that you had better do some quick research.

If you think that it would be best to ask Mrs. Puddington these questions, turn to page 109.

If you decide to go to the local library to look through back issues of the Plumtown Gazette, turn to page 56.

The three of you drive out to the railroad trestle at Campbell Creek. Followed by you and IQ, Stretch hurries down the embankment.

As Stretch approaches the tool shed, he motions for both of you to stand back. With his hand on his revolver, he cautiously opens the door of the shed.

The shed is empty. But as you follow Stretch inside, you smell cigar smoke. Lying in an ashtray on a small table is a burning cigar. "Judging by the length of the ash, we've missed our man by fifteen minutes," you say.

"You're right," IQ says. "And Mr. Blackburne left in a hurry. The other cigar butts in the ashtray have been carefully put out. It's not this man's practice to leave one burning like this."

"Maybe Waldorf finally caught up with him and told him that we were looking for him," you say.

"Good guess," says Stretch. "Let's check for other clues."

You examine the rest of the shed. It appears that Blackburne has been staying here for some time: a large plastic bag filled with empty cans and ice-cream cartons is propped against one wall.

"There is plenty of evidence to suggest that he was holed up here," IQ observes, "but there are no personal items—no socks, no change of clothes, no razor. When Blackburne left here, he wasn't planning to come back."

"You're right, IQ," Stretch says.

"That's because the kidnapping will take place at tonight's game," you say.

"It's an hour to game time," Stretch says, turning to you, "and I think you should play. Having you stand around on the sidelines might alert the plotters. They must have been checking out these games for a while. They'd know you're one of the starters."

"I know that," you say, "but maybe we should trace that phone number first."

Back at the car, Stretch gets on his police radio and asks the operator at headquarters to run the telephone number through a police computer. In about three minutes he has an answer. He signs off and turns to you and IQ.

"It's Jastrow Peevler of 301 Elm Street," says Stretch. "He's a well-known troublemaker. We have to move fast. What do you think is our best move?"

If you decide to get to the game on time, turn to page 51.

If you want to go to Peevler's address first, turn to page 111.

"Run!" you say in a hushed voice. "Dynamite taped to the trestle!"

You have spotted a charge of dynamite secured to the side of the trestle with heavy tape.

The three of you race back toward the road. But the sound of running has alerted the two criminals. Peevler rushes into the tool shed, where he detonates the charge.

The three of you have just reached the end of the trestle as the charge explodes. You, Stretch, and IQ are thrown to the ground by the force of the blast and showered with debris. You hear the trestle collapse as all goes black.

It is an hour before you regain consciousness, and Stretch and IQ are still out. You have no doubt foiled the kidnapping plot. The blowing-up of the bridge was obviously planned as a diversion to occur during the abduction of Cappy Wiltburrow, but the charge has gone off prematurely. Peevler and his accomplice have escaped, however, leaving them free to strike again somewhere else.

THE END

Chandler School
Goshen, Indiana

from page 36

You go back to the scene of the struggle. Down on one knee, you examine the ground for clues. You might find something that will give you a lead.

You push aside some broken branches. There on the ground, half-covered by a leaf, you spot a small button. You put it into your pocket. It may have been torn from the kidnapper's shirt by Cappy Wiltburrow.

You look for other clues, but find none at the same spot. Now you take a look around a wider area. You locate the point where the kidnappers seem to have gone off the path. From there you can see a long trail where the underbrush has been flattened.

Most likely, you guess, Cappy was carried away through the woods to a point on the road much farther down from where Gifford was waiting with the limo. An accomplice probably waited there with the get-away car.

You follow the trail for about ten yards, looking for anything at all that might give you a lead. Suddenly, you smell something—a burning cigar. Then you spot the thick, half-smoked cigar lying next to a large rock. You pick it up between two fingers and snuff it out. You wrap it in a large, green maple leaf and put it in your pocket.

Now you have a couple of clues. At least there is

something to work with. You also realize that if Gifford has done as you asked, Stretch should be arriving
at the ball field right about now. You've got to decide
quickly what you are going to do.

*If you follow the trail through the underbrush, hoping
to find new clues, turn to page 68.*

*If you return to the ball field to meet Stretch, turn to
page 69.*

Stretch drives you back to your house, where you change quickly into your baseball uniform. Then he leaves to set up a police stakeout at the ball field. IQ goes home to pick up his binoculars.

You go to the game and play center field for the Cowboys. Cappy Wiltburrow plays the same position for the opposing team, the Braves.

The game is exciting. Each team gets a lot of hits and scores several runs. By the end of five innings, the score is tied at nine all.

In the top of the sixth inning, Cappy Wiltburrow gets a base on balls. The next batter bunts him over to second base. Then the third batter lines a single up the middle.

You charge the ball, field it smoothly, and make an excellent throw to the plate. But Cappy's courageous head-first slide beats your throw by inches.

Billy Kroger, you team's catcher, is alert. He quickly throws the ball to second base to catch the runner, who took too wide a turn around the bag. The next two batters strike out, so your team comes up in the bottom of the last inning trailing the Braves by a run.

The first batter for your team hits a wicked line drive, but right at the Brave's shortstop. One out. The next batter strikes out on three pitches.

With one out left, Billy Kroger steps up to the plate. You are on deck. You look up into the stands at IQ, who shrugs his shoulders. He hasn't seen anything unusual through his binoculars.

Billy takes two pitches, a ball and a strike. Then he crowds the plate. The opposing pitcher, attempting to brush him back, grazes Billy's arm with the next pitch. The umpire awards Billy first base.

Now it's up to you. You step to the plate and take several hard practice swings.

The first pitch is a curve that breaks below your knees. Ball one. The next pitch comes in hard, down the middle. You swing a little late and foul it into the backstop. You can see that the pitcher is bearing down. He is trying too hard, however. The next pitch goes in the dirt.

The count stands at two balls, one strike. You dig in and crowd the plate, but the pitcher won't let you get away with that. He throws a chest-high fastball that brushes you back. The count goes to three and one.

You know that you've been set up for a pitch over the outside corner, but you are not going to swing at it. Even if it is a strike, you don't think it will be a good pitch to hit.

Just as you expected, the pitch is on the outside corner. "Strike two," the umpire calls.

The count is full at three and two. You've faced this pitcher before. He doesn't believe in walking the winning run. You expect his hardest fastball down the middle. This guy will challenge you. "Let him," you think.

You get ready. You plant your feet square to the plate, and clench your teeth. The pitcher rears back and fires.

There it is—your pitch. A flat fastball in your power zone. Your swing is perfect and you connect.

You've stroked a mighty drive. The left and center fielders both race to deep left-center field, but the ball is gone, sailing high over the outstretched glove of Cappy Wiltburrow.

You break into your home-run trot around the bases. The crowd cheers wildly and your teammates gather near home plate, ready to mob you as you cross with the winning run.

But as soon as you step down on the plate, you turn around toward the field. Through the bobbing heads and excited waving arms of your teammates, you see a dejected Cappy Wiltburrow leave the field by the gate near third base. He turns and starts to walk along the outside of the fence toward the woods.

Pulling yourself away from your teammates, you move in Cappy's direction. You turn and look back up into the stands for IQ. His binoculars are trained on the path that Cappy will take through the woods. The limousine should be waiting on the other side.

You shout to get IQ's attention, and he sees you.

IQ points frantically in the direction of the path, and you begin to trot after Cappy. He is already a fair distance away from you. Where, you wonder, is Sergeant Stretch? Cappy is already disappearing into the woods, and there is no sign of Stretch's stakeout.

The situation calls for a quick decision.

If you choose to avoid the path and move out toward the road, turn to page 61.

If you choose to race into the woods after Cappy, turn to page 64.

You and Stretch sit back and relax. It's probably not important that there is something suspicious about Waldorf. Stretch agrees with you that your nerves are probably just on edge.

You wait about five minutes, then Waldorf opens the door to the sitting room and steps in.

"I've discussed the whole matter of Master Cappy's kidnapping with...my friends, Mr. Peevler and Mr. Blackburne," Waldorf says.

Two men step into the room. They hold revolvers, which they are pointing at you and Stretch.

"This is what my two friends would call—oh, how do you say it, Jastrow?" Waldorf says smartly.

"Tough luck," says the lean, sunken-cheeked thug.

"Yeah, real tough luck for you and the kid, copper," says the other thug, an out-of-towner known to the underworld as Bronco Blackburne.

"But just a moment," Waldorf says. "Let me leave first. You know how I hate gunplay and...the sight of blood," the butler says as he closes the door behind him.

THE END

You go to the library and spend almost an hour and a half of precious time scanning microfilm of old Plumtown *Gazettes*. You are ready to give up and leave. Game time is drawing near.

But as you view what you've decided will be the last roll of microfilm, your eye catches a headline that you can hardly believe. You quickly read the entire story, then you look for further coverage of the matter in later *Gazettes*.

The news story that you have discovered was printed thirty years ago. Now you understand the meaning of the word grudge. As you search further, different names and events fit together like pieces of a puzzle.

There's no time to waste now, however. You've got to find IQ, and also get in touch with Sergeant Stretch of the Plumtown Police.

First you return to the baseball diamond to look for IQ. You leave your bicycle in the woods. Then you walk around to all the logical places that IQ might have chosen to keep an eye on Big Martin, the groundskeeper.

You can see that Big Martin is still out on the field, just now putting down the white chalk baselines. You can't find IQ, though. Doing your best to stay out of Big Martin's sight, you continue your search.

The Plumtown Gaz[ette]

June 15, 1954

RISCILLA PUDDI[NG]
WED F. G. WILTBU[RY]

Then you see something that makes your heart sink. IQ's bicycle lies twisted and smashed against a rock in the woods beyond center field. Your greatest fear is that your friend IQ has been hurt. You check the bicycle and the nearby area for clues.

You find nothing, but you know you must solve this case to find out what happened to IQ. You've got two phone calls to make. The first one is to Sergeant Stretch. The second is to Mrs. Puddington. You run back to where you left your bicycle, then pedal to the nearest pay phone.

"Sergeant Stretch, please," you say when the police operator answers.

"Stretch speaking," you hear when you are connected.

You quickly give Stretch a background briefing on your investigation up to this point. You leave out only a few pieces of the puzzle about which you are still unsure. Stretch tells you that he is impressed by the thoroughness of your work.

You tell him that you think Cappy Wiltburrow will be safe, and that IQ can be found, if you solve the case tonight before the game. You ask him to pick up Jastrow Peevler for questioning and bring him to the baseball clubhouse. You also ask Stretch if he can see to it that Waldorf, the Wiltburrow butler, is there as well.

"O.K., kid," Stretch says. "Just be careful."

"I will be," you say.

Next you call Mrs. Puddington.

"Good heavens, dear," she says when she hears your voice, "I have been waiting all day for your call. What have you discovered?"

"I think I've got the case solved, Mrs. Puddington," you say. "Can you make it down to the baseball clubhouse before tonight's game? I need your help."

She hesitates for a second before answering you.

"Why, yes," Mrs. Puddington says, "I shall be happy to meet you there. I shall ring up my driver right now and have him bring the car around."

"Thank you," you say. "I'll see you there."

You get back on your bicycle and head off to the clubhouse. You look around for Big Martin Broadaxe, and you see him far down the left-field line near the fence. You let yourself into the clubhouse with the key you hold as captain of your baseball team.

You walk into the glass office inside the clubhouse where all the league records are kept. Opening one of the file drawers, you pull out a folder marked "Martin Broadaxe, employment records."

You quickly go through the contents of the folder, remove a few items, and then return the folder to the file. You look at the clock on the clubhouse wall.

Twenty minutes remain until people start showing up for your little gathering.

You wonder if you should confront Big Martin now about IQ, or just invite him to the gathering. You are concerned for IQ's safety, but it might be best to take one thing at a time.

If you decide to ask Martin Broadaxe to attend the gathering, turn to page 72.

If you decide to confront Martin before the gathering, turn to page 85.

You veer off the path and make a wide circle through the woods. You don't want to disrupt Stretch's stakeout. But you are still puzzled. Where is Stretch?

When you reach the road, you spot the waiting Wiltburrow limousine. The chauffeur is standing on the shoulder of the road, trying to see through the trees and into the woods. He seems worried.

You jog toward him and he turns in your direction. You speak first.

"Has anything happened?"

"What?" the chauffeur says.

"Have you seen any police officers?"

"No, I haven't seen any police officers," he says with irritation, "nor have I seen Master Cappy."

All this is peculiar. Where are Stretch and the other police officers? Is Cappy Wiltburrow all right?

You decide to wait another five minutes before going back into the woods to find out for yourself. You check your watch. The five minutes seem to take forever, but nothing happens.

Finally you run down the path into the woods. You see nothing at first, but as you continue along, you spot a pair of feet sticking out into the path.

It's Stretch! He's bound and gagged. You quickly untie him.

"They've gotten away," he says. "They have Cappy. I blew it. Blackburne dynamited the trestle over Campbell Creek. Practically our entire police force went out there, so there was no one around to help me. I thought I could handle it on my own."

You help Stretch look for his gun, which Blackburne had thrown into the bushes. Just as you find the gun, you see IQ walking toward you. In a hurry, you explain to him what has happened.

"You forget," IQ says, "that Jastrow Peevler may be involved in this, and we know where he lives."

"Right," you say.

The three of you race back to where Stretch had parked his car.

Almost forty minutes have passed since Blackburne and an accomplice abducted Cappy Wiltburrow. Stretch turns on his siren and puts a flashing red light on the car roof. At the same time, he radios headquarters to send available squad cars to Peevler's residence.

Your car and two other squad cars arrive at 301 Elm Street at the same time. The officers spread out to cover the house from all angles. Stretch pulls a bullhorn out of the trunk of his car and speaks into it.

"All right, you two, let the kid go, and then both of you come out with your hands up."

There is no answer.

The officers surrounding the house slowly close in. Then, with his gun drawn, one officer carefully approaches the house and enters.

As you watch, the officer comes back out waving his arms. Blackburne and Peevler have flown the coop and taken Cappy with them.

You all search the house for further clues but find none. Later, you find out that Waldorf, the Wiltburrow butler, has also disappeared.

A few months go by. The Wiltburrows close down their mansion and leave Plumtown. Then one day you read in the newspaper that Cappy Wiltburrow was returned to his family. The FBI, the story says, is still searching for the kidnappers. You can only assume that Cappy's father, Frederick G. Wiltburrow, was forced to pay thousands of dollars in ransom money.

Bronco Blackburne and Jastrow Peevler have combined luck and cunning to pull off a successful kidnapping. No doubt they have both changed their identities and now live in the lap of luxury.

If only I had heeded my instincts, you think, and followed Cappy into the woods. We might have stopped them. But at least Cappy is safe now.

THE END

64

from page 54

It's hard to believe that Stretch wouldn't give you a sign if everything was O.K. Something must be wrong. Disregarding your own safety, you race into the woods after Cappy.

Approaching a sharp turn in the path, you hear muffled cries. You get down on your stomach and crawl forward. You can see two men tightening ropes around the ankles and wrists of a gagged Cappy Wiltburrow!

The men lift Cappy and carry him off into the woods, away from the path that leads to the waiting limousine. As they rush off, you crawl forward again. Suddenly you see two bound, kicking feet that stick out into the path from the bush near where Cappy was abducted.

Behind the bush you find an embarrassed Sergeant Stretch, bound and gagged. You quickly untie your friend.

"I walked right into it," says Stretch. "By the time I got back to headquarters, every available officer had been sent up to the railroad trestle at Campbell Creek. Blackburne must have set off an explosive up there as a diversion. We left there just a half hour before it went off. I had to come here alone, and Blackburne must have been waiting for me. He took my gun and threw it into the bushes."

"I'll find it," you say as you scramble into the bushes. You quickly fish out Stretch's revolver and hand it to him.

Racing after the kidnappers, you and Stretch reach a point far down the road from the parked Wiltburrow limousine. You get there in time to see a car disappear over a rise about a hundred yards away.

"We've lost them," Stretch says.

Suddenly a voice startles you both.

"You are forgetting about Jastrow Peevler," says IQ, stepping onto the side of the road from the woods.

"IQ!" you say. "You're right!"

Stretch leads you and IQ back to the car. Then you all drive at high speed toward 301 Elm Street, Peevler's address.

Taking the most obvious route might scare Peevler into making a break for it. So Stretch drives up from the opposite end of Elm Street.

Stretch pulls over to the curb several doors from Peevler's house. "Wait here for five minutes," he tells you and IQ, "then create a disturbance in front of the house. Make lots of noise. Let's see what happens."

Stretch walks quickly to the rear of a house on the same side of Elm Street as Peevler's house. Moving like a cat, he disappears into the back yard.

You and IQ wait five minutes, then walk down the sidewalk. You stop in front of Peevler's house.

"You played a lousy game," IQ shouts at you.

"I played how?" you shout back.

Then the two of you begin a pretend pushing-and-shouting match. You are both very loud.

Less than a minute later, the front door of Peevler's house opens. Out walk Bronco Blackburne and Jastrow Peevler, with their hands high above their heads. They are followed by Sergeant Stretch, his gun drawn, and a pale Cappy Wiltburrow.

"Thanks," Stretch says to you as he ushers the two scowling criminals toward his police car. "I got in the back door while these fellows were distracted by your shouting."

"No problem," you say.

"Hey, why don't you guys see that Cappy gets home O.K.," says Stretch.

With that, you and IQ and Cappy walk off in the opposite direction. You and IQ make jokes about the bumbling kidnappers, and after a few minutes you have Cappy laughing along with you.

THE END

from page 50

The fresh trail through the woods is too much for you to ignore. You walk along quickly, your eyes scanning the ground for more clues.

The trail curves around a large rock as big as a pickup truck. About ten feet on the other side of the rock, you spot something on the ground. It looks like a baseball cap, partially hidden by the underbrush.

You stop and reach down for it.

Without any warning, a large burlap sack comes flying down over your head and shoulders.

A hand presses against your face through the burlap. The hand holds something with a deep chemical smell. It's ether, you think, as your mind goes numb and fades into blackness.

THE END

from page 50

Sergeant Stretch of the Plumtown Police is just pulling into the parking lot next to the ball field. You walk over to meet him.

"They've kidnapped Cappy Wiltburrow, Sarge," you say.

"So I hear," Stretch says, slamming the door of his squad car behind him.

You tell Stretch all that you know, from the fragment of conversation that you overheard last night to the burning cigar you found in the woods.

"I think we'd better go out and inform Mr. Wiltburrow before we do anything else," Stretch says.

"I think you're right," you say.

You and Stretch hop into the car and drive out to Wiltburrow Manor.

A few seconds after Stretch rings the bell, the front door is opened by Waldorf, the Wiltburrow family butler.

"May I help you?" Waldorf asks.

"Stretch, of the Plumtown Police," the Sergeant says, holding up his police shield and identification. "Is Mr. Wiltburrow in?"

"Why no, sir," Waldorf says. "Mr. Wiltburrow is out of town on business. Mrs. Wiltburrow is with him."

"Well, that's unfortunate," Stretch says. "We have a serious matter here. Can you contact the Wiltburrows at their hotel? Their son, Cappy, has been kidnapped."

Waldorf's face registers shock at the news. For a few seconds, he cannot speak.

"Yes, of course, Sergeant," Waldorf says. "Come right in. I will get in touch with Mr. Wiltburrow immediately."

You follow Stretch into the magnificent Wiltburrow mansion. Waldorf leads you to a large sitting room.

"I will call Mr. Wiltburrow now," Waldorf says, as he leaves the room.

"We must move quickly," Stretch tells Waldorf.

As soon as Waldorf is gone, you lean over and whisper in Stretch's ear, filling him in on some of the things that you've noticed.

If you wait for Waldorf to return, turn to page 55.

If you decide to follow Waldorf to see what he is up to, turn to page 81.

72

from page 60

There is no sense, you think, in risking a confrontation with Big Martin now. Stretch will be here soon, and you now believe the groundskeeper, though dangerous, plays only a minor role in the kidnapping plot. You must not allow your concern for IQ to force you into acting rashly.

A few minutes remain before you expect people to start arriving at the clubhouse. You walk outside and onto the ball field near home plate. Big Martin is still out by the left-field foul pole. Cupping your hands around your mouth, you yell out to get his attention. He looks in your direction.

"Come down to the clubhouse when you get a chance," you yell.

Big Martin lowers his head and goes back to what he was doing, without acknowledging you.

"Just as well," you say to yourself. You know that he's not going anywhere.

You go back inside the clubhouse and arrange five chairs in a wide semicircle, leaving plenty of room between each one.

Just as you finish, you hear the clubhouse door open. In walks the menacing Bronco Blackburne.

"Hello, Blackburne," you say. "Why don't you have a seat?"

"Sure," he growls. "I'll have a seat."

As he sits down, Stretch arrives with the wretched Jastrow Peevler, whom he has had to put in handcuffs.

"Hi, kid," says Stretch. "Here's one of the packages you requested. The other one, Waldorf, will be delivered by one of my men."

"Have a seat, Mr. Peevler," you say.

Shortly, Stretch's man arrives with Waldorf, just before Big Martin Broadaxe lumbers in from the field.

Now you await only the arrival of Mrs. Puddington, who is a few minutes late. Blackburne, Peevler, Waldorf, and Big Martin sit in silence. They do not look at one another.

Finally, the elegant Mrs. Puddington enters the clubhouse.

"My dear," she says, "it is so good to see you safe and sound. I'm so glad I can be of help."

"Thank you for coming, Mrs. Puddington," you say. "Why don't you have a seat, and we can begin."

As Mrs. Puddington sits down, Stretch moves over to cover the door. His man waits outside. And you are ready to unravel the plot.

"In case you do not know why we are here, let me explain," you begin. "In the first place, I have become aware of a plot to kidnap young Casper Wiltburrow, known to his friends as 'Cappy.' Second, and now of even greater importance, we are here to solve the disappearance of my close friend and colleague, James Peters, known to most of his friends as 'IQ.' "

"Get on with it kid, you're wastin' my time," Blackburne barks.

"Pipe down, Bronco," Stretch says.

"Thank you, Sergeant. Mr. Blackburne," you continue, "it was you I saw last night in the woods beyond this ball field."

"Prove it, kid. Nobody could see nothin' last night," Blackburne says.

Stretch hears this and nods at you, a slight smile creasing his face.

"I don't have to prove it," you say, "because Mr. Peevler will vouch for your presence in the woods. He was there with you. Weren't you, Mr. Peevler?"

"I ain't sayin' nothing," Peevler says.

"Well that's O.K., too, Mr. Peevler," you say, "because in order to lighten his own sentence for conspiracy to kidnap a minor, Mr. Martin Broadaxe will happily tell us about how he became involved in the plot."

"He forced me into it," Big Martin shouts, jumping to his feet and pointing at Peevler. "He threatened to have me fired!"

Stretch moves over to the groundskeeper and quickly gets him back in his seat.

"Well, Mr. Peevler, Mr. Broadaxe certainly seems to have implicated you. So I'm sure that Mr. Blackburne would like to follow suit and admit you also hired *him*."

"Yeah," Blackburne shouts, "he paid me to work out the details of the plan."

"You rat," Peevler shouts.

"Settle down, you two," Stretch says in a tough voice.

"But what is behind all this?" you say. "Surely Mr. Peevler and Mr. Blackburne are capable of many things, but why kidnapping? Why such a serious crime? Do you have an answer for us, Mr. Peevler?"

"Yeah," Peevler says. "I have an answer."

"Jastrow!" Mrs. Puddington shouts.

Peevler shuts his mouth, and Mrs. Puddington looks around the room with an embarrassed expression on her face. You look over at Stretch, who looks back at you with surprise.

"The motive behind this plot," you say, "was not a large ransom. The motive was and is *revenge*, revenge against Cappy's father, Frederick G. Wiltburrow, for an offense committed nearly thirty years ago.

"You see," you continue, "long before Mr. Wilt-

Chandler School
Goshen, Indiana

burrow met Cappy's mother, he had once made plans to marry another woman. Those plans were big news in Plumtown, but Mr. Wiltburrow canceled them, and called off the wedding."

You walk across the room and stand next to Mrs. Puddington, who has buried her face in her hands.

"But the woman," you say, "whom Mr. Wiltburrow did not marry has never forgotten. And she has never forgiven him. Recently, she had her distant cousin, whom she supports with a tiny allowance, set in motion a plan to abduct her former suitor's pride and joy, his youngest son, Cappy. The distant cousin is our friend Mr. Peevler, who in turn hired Mr. Blackburne to be the chief thug. He also threatened Martin Broadaxe with the loss of his job if he did not cooperate as well.

"Where," you ask, "did Jastrow get the power to threaten Martin Broadaxe's job? From the woman who recommended Broadaxe to the baseball league, the woman who had once employed the groundskeeper as a part-time gardener. And that woman is the same woman who is Mr. Peevler's cousin, who is the same woman Cappy Wiltburrow's father had once intended to marry. That woman is you, Mrs. Puddington," you say as you turn to her.

Priscilla Puddington is now sobbing loudly. You have always liked her, and now you feel sorry for her.

But you know that she is vengeful and ruthless, and that she sent you after Peevler, Broadaxe, and Blackburne this morning with the certainty that one of them would get you out of the way.

"Now, Mr. Broadaxe, would you tell us where we can find my friend IQ?"

"He's tied up in the shed where I keep my equipment. But he's O.K. He just has a bruise from when I knocked him off his bicycle."

"Thank you," you say, "and thank you, Waldorf. I think that you were probably being set up to look like the guilty party. Are you missing any of your clothing, or a pair of shoes?"

"Why, yes," Waldorf says, "my old pair of oxfords is gone."

"They're probably in the possession of Mr. Peevler or Mr. Blackburne. It would have been your shoe prints that were found at the scene of the crime."

"Great work, kid," Stretch says.

"Thanks, Sarge," you say as you turn to leave.

"Where are you going?" he asks.

"I think I'd better let IQ out of the shed. He doesn't like confined spaces."

THE END

from page 10

The three of you drive over to the Plumtown Bijou. The woman who runs the box office has just arrived to go over last night's receipts and to prepare for today's matinee.

She invites you to sit down in the lobby. Stretch nods his head, giving you the O.K. to ask questions.

"I know this may be difficult ma'am," you say, "but try to remember back a few nights ago. There was a man who bought a ticket to the movie and then complained loudly about the price. His voice was high-pitched and nasal."

The woman squints her eyes, putting her hand to her forehead. "I think I do remember," she says. "Yes, he was very rude, and I've seen him here before. We haven't raised the price of tickets for four years, but he complained as though we were raising them every week."

"Can you remember what he looked like?" you ask.

"Well," she says, "let me think. His face was long and thin, I recall, and he had kind of sunken cheeks, and, oh yes, his hair was very greasy, as though he'd overdone it with his hair tonic."

"Wait a minute," Stretch says, "that sounds like Jastrow Peevler, and this is exactly the kind of thing I'd expect him to be involved in."

"Peevler," IQ says. "I've read about him in the newspaper."

"Yes," you say, "he's a notorious gambler and con artist."

"That's right," Stretch says. "We've hauled him in several times, but we could never get enough evidence to make any of the charges stick. He's a slippery character."

"What's our next move?" IQ asks.

You decide to consult your contacts at the Plumtown Billiard Hall.

Turn to page 83.

from page 71

You and Stretch quietly follow Waldorf. You see him enter another room, at the end of a long, carpeted hallway.

Stretch looks at you with an expression that tells you he senses something fishy.

You and he walk up to the door and listen. You hear more than one voice—Waldorf's, and those of two other men.

"Well," Stretch whispers, "I can't really hear what they're saying, but the butler isn't calling Mr. Wiltburrow, is he?"

You nod at Stretch in agreement. Then he pulls his police revolver from inside his coat and opens the kitchen door.

"Nobody move!" he shouts.

Three men slowly raise their hands over their heads. You rush over and untie Cappy Wiltburrow and IQ, who are both bound to chairs and gagged.

"I guess this was really an inside job. Right, Waldorf?" Stretch says.

The plan had been beautifully designed. With Cappy's parents away on a trip, the family butler teamed up with a couple of thugs. They planned to grab the kid and hold him for a huge ransom. Maybe they would even have let Cappy go, once they had the money and were out of the country.

It's just plain luck that you and IQ went star-gazing last night, and uncovered the plot to kidnap Cappy Wiltburrow. But it was your good detective work that saved the day.

THE END

from page 80

When you get to the Plumtown Billiard Hall, Stretch and IQ wait outside. The guys in the place don't like police, but they trust you.

You walk in and say hello to Bob Brown, the manager.

"Hiya, Bob," you say.

"What's up, kid?" he replies.

"Have you seen the Ear?"

"Yeah, sure, the Ear's back there," he says, pointing to the back room.

In the back room, you find the Ear sitting off to the side, watching two men shoot pool.

"Hey, Earful," you say, using the more familiar form of his nickname.

"Hello, kid, what can I do for you?"

You gesture to him with your palm down, a signal that the conversation should be kept at a whisper.

"What can you tell me about Jastrow Peevler?" you ask.

"Hey listen, kid, Peevler's somebody you don't want to mess with. He's nothing but trouble."

"I already know that much. But I'm safe, believe me. I need any information you might have. It could be a matter of life and death."

"O.K., kid," the Ear says, "but don't say I didn't warn you. Peevler's been very nervous lately. The boys think he's about to pull off a big job. Nobody listens too close, because they don't want to hear anything that could get them hurt. But the latest word is that he's been mixing up some trouble at Campbell Creek, something to do with the railroad trestle.

"That's all I know, kid, honest Injun. And don't ever tell anyone you heard it here," the Ear says.

"You have my word," you say.

You rejoin Sergeant Stretch and IQ, who are waiting in the car.

"Let's head out to the railroad trestle at Campbell Creek. I think we've got a hot tip."

Stretch starts the car, makes a U-turn, and heads out of town toward the trestle. On the way, you relay the vague information you got from the Ear, remembering not to mention his name.

As you near the trestle, you must decide how you are going to approach this.

If you want to walk out onto the trestle to look for something out of the ordinary, turn to page 86.

If you want to climb down the embankment and check out an abandoned tool shed, turn to page 96.

from page 60

You are certain that Big Martin Broadaxe, the groundskeeper, has abducted IQ. Stretch will soon be on the scene, so you decide to get things started. You walk out onto the ball field.

Big Martin is still out by the left-field foul pole. You head down the left-field line, with your shoulders squared and a determined expression on your face.

When you get to about ten feet from where Broadaxe is standing, you stop. His back is to you. "All right, Mr. Broadaxe," you say. "Where is my friend?"

The big groundskeeper turns around slowly. His face is full of guilt. He holds a large burlap sack, into which he has been putting grass clippings.

"O.K.," he says sadly, "I'll take you to him."

"Let's go," you say. "You lead the way."

Big Martin Broadaxe lumbers forward, his head hanging so that his chin rests on his chest.

Suddenly, just as he passes you, he turns and throws the burlap sack over your head and shoulders.

"I've been waitin' for you," you hear Broadaxe say as all goes dark.

THE END

86

Stretch parks the car about a hundred feet from the trestle. The three of you walk cautiously toward it, your eyes open for any sign of trouble. No one else is around.

You walk carefully out onto the trestle, stepping on the railroad ties. Stretch leans over the side and looks down at the tool shed. Then he looks at you and IQ, holding a finger to his lips to warn you to be quiet.

The three of you peep down over the side. Sixty feet below are two men standing outside the shed. They are talking, but you can't make out what they are saying.

"The one on the left is Peevler," says Stretch.

"And the other one is large enough to be the big guy I saw by the ball field last night."

"We should make our move soon," IQ whispers.

Suddenly, you spot something that makes you react instantly. A split-second decision is called for.

If you stay on the trestle to try to deal with what you have seen, turn to page 91.

If you rush everyone off the railroad trestle, turn to page 47.

from page 26

The name Jastrow Peevler alone makes you suspicious. A hunch tells you to check him out now, before you investigate Blackburne.

First you ride your bicycle home and pick up your magazine sales kit. You've got to have an excuse to knock on someone's door. Jastrow Peevler must think that you are selling magazines door-to-door to earn extra money.

With sales kit in hand, you pedal your way over to Elm Street. Peevler's house is number 301.

You park your bicycle on the sidewalk and walk confidently up the front path. Peevler's house is a mess. It doesn't appear to have had a paint job in a decade.

You knock on the front door and wait. Several seconds later, a thin man with sunken cheeks and dirty hair opens the door.

"Yeah?" he says.

"Good morning, sir," you say, holding up your sales kit. "Could I interest you in subscriptions to some very fine magazines?"

"Sure, sure, I love magazines," Peevler says enthusiastically. "Come right in."

You didn't think it would be this easy. Peevler opens his door all the way and lets you walk in.

"Now," you say, opening your sales kit, "let me

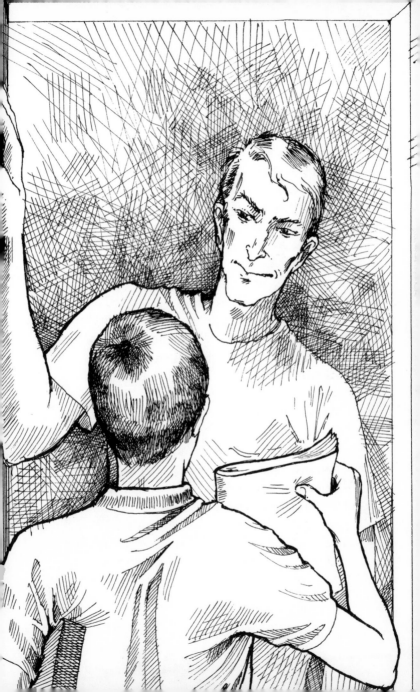

show you what I have and explain the various purchase plans."

"Oh, of course," Peevler says. "I want to know all about that. But could you do me a favor, kid? My reading glasses are in the other room over there, just on the other side of that door."

"That door," you say, pointing.

"Yes," Peevler says. "In there on my desk. Would you grab them for me? The light switch is on the far wall."

"Sure," you say helpfully.

You walk over to the door and open it. The room is totally dark, so you carefully make your way toward the far wall, feeling for the light switch.

You find the switch. Just as you turn on the light, you see Peevler standing at the door.

"Who do you think you're kidding, kid?" he says as he slams the door.

You see that you are in an empty, windowless room. You've fallen into a trap, and you know that you'll be here until someone finds you. There is no way to get out. You hope that IQ will be able to rescue you.

THE END

from page 86

What you have seen is a charge of dynamite secured with heavy tape to the side of the trestle. If Peevler and his accomplice were to see the three of you running, they could detonate the dynamite before you made it off the trestle to safety.

You lie down and reach through the girders of the trestle platform. You can just barely reach the charge.

As you begin to peel off the tape, you look down. Your eyes lock with the vicious eyes of Jastrow Peevler. You both freeze for a second, then Peevler rushes into the shed. You know that he intends to detonate the charge!

You struggle to yank the dynamite from the side of the trestle. Beads of sweat break out across your forehead. With one last desperate pull, you rip the dynamite from the steel and let it drop.

"Cover your heads," you shout to Stretch and IQ as you curl yourself into a ball.

The charge detonates just above the tool shed. Flying dust and debris engulf all three of you, but you remain unhurt.

Stretch leads you and IQ off the trestle. You are all coughing from the dust.

"Good work," says Stretch, "you saved our lives. They must have planned to blow up the trestle as a diversion. Then they would have had an easy time grabbing young Wiltburrow."

"That was their plan," IQ says.

You and IQ watch as Stretch goes down the embankment to arrest the scared and dirty criminals, who survived the blast. Minutes later they confess their plan, and Cappy Wiltburrow's safety is secured.

THE END

Leaving your admiring teammates behind, you bolt from the field and head for the area behind the bleachers. You stand there and look in every direction for a sign of IQ.

You are still deciding what you must do, when someone taps you on the shoulder. Turning around with a start, you find yourself face-to-face with Big Martin Broadaxe, the groundskeeper of the ball field.

"Are you looking for your friend with the binoculars?" he asks you.

"Yes, have you see him?" you ask.

"Come with me," Big Martin says as he turns and walks away.

You follow him down the outside of the fence that runs along the left-field line. You are anxious to reach IQ, but Big Martin moves slowly.

Finally, you reach the shed where you know Big Martin keeps his groundskeeping equipment. He fumbles with his keys and then unlocks the shed.

"Your friend is hiding in here," he says.

You lean into the dark shed. You see two feet sticking out from behind a large roll of plastic that is used to cover home plate and the batting area.

"IQ?" you yell.

Suddenly a large hand shoves you into the shed.

Then Big Martin Broadaxe closes the door behind him and shines a huge flashlight in your face. The next thing you know, he covers your mouth with adhesive tape and ties your hands and legs. You may be in this shed for a long time.

THE END

from page 34

You pedal your bicycle furiously as you rush back to the ball field. You must get IQ to back you up when you confront Blackburne.

IQ has been quietly watching Big Martin Broadaxe, the groundskeeper, and you don't want to give your friend away. You ride around the outskirts of the ball field, looking for IQ's observation post.

Suddenly, you come to a dead stop. There on the ground, behind a big rock, are IQ's glasses. You get down from your bicycle and lean over to pick them up.

As you stand back up, you look out over the field. You are in the woods beyond the right-field fence. You see the large, lumbering figure of Big Martin Broadaxe on the other side of the field. He is dragging a bulging sack toward a gate in the fence.

You must act quickly, on your own, because IQ's life may be at stake.

Turn to page 101.

from page 84

Stretch parks the car a fair distance from the trestle. The three of you walk quickly and quietly the rest of the way. Then Stretch takes the lead as he walks carefully down the steep embankment.

When you reach the bottom, Stretch looks around, then moves toward the tool shed. Just as Stretch pauses to reach under his jacket for his revolver, Jastrow Peevler swings around from behind the shed and aims a gun at Stretch's forehead.

"Up with those hands, copper," Peevler demands. "Come on out, Bronco."

As Stretch reluctantly reaches upward, the frightening figure of Bronco Blackburne emerges from the shed. He points his gun at you and IQ.

"All right, all of you, into the shed and down on your knees," Peevler says menacingly.

The three of you walk into the shed. You all get on your knees as ordered, then Peevler ties rope around your wrists and ankles. He puts thick adhesive tape across your mouths.

"That should hold them," Peevler says.

"Just long enough," Blackburne replies with a laugh.

Just before the crooks close the door on you, Peevler adds, "You guys will be right where the action is when the trestle blows up. And while your fellow cops are out here wasting their time investigating, we'll be grabbing the million-dollar kid, Cappy Wiltburrow."

"So long," says Peevler as he closes the door to the shed. You, IQ, and Stretch are left in darkness.

THE END

from page 36

You run back down the path. A horrible feeling in your stomach tells you that IQ is in great danger. You think someone who is involved in the plot must have seen IQ watching the woods with binoculars. That person may have tricked IQ and led him into a trap.

As you round the corner of the fence outside deep left field, you notice that Big Martin Broadaxe, the groundskeeper, is putting a large padlock on the door of his equipment shed. It sounds as if he is talking to himself.

You hide on the other side of the shed.

"Just be quiet in there, and nothing will happen to you," you hear Big Martin say.

You guess that the groundskeeper is speaking to your friend IQ. Big Martin is in league with the kidnappers!

How do you handle this?

If you wait for Sergeant Stretch to arrive, turn to page 104.

If you try to free IQ yourself, turn to page 7.

from page 23

As Stretch and IQ drive away, you slip back into the Wiltburrow mansion through an open window.

Letting your instincts guide you from room to room, you listen at each door for the sound of Waldorf's voice. Within a few minutes you come to the right door. You hear Waldorf talking to someone over the phone.

You gently push open the door so that you can hear what the butler is saying.

"...but I think that they must have heard something, gotten wind of our plot from somewhere," Waldorf says. He pauses for a second to listen, and then he continues.

"No, Mr. Peevler, it is not my imagination. They were here in plain sight—accompanied by a police officer. They spoke of our plot to Mr. Wiltburrow just fifteen minutes ago."

You've heard enough. You hurry to rejoin Stretch and IQ, who are waiting for you outside the main gate.

You tell Stretch the story, and he quickly turns the car around. He accelerates back up the drive to Wiltburrow Manor. With lights flashing and siren blasting, the car screeches to a halt at the front door of the mansion.

You ring the doorbell. When there is no answer, the three of you put your shoulders to the door and force it open.

A few seconds later you catch Waldorf attempting to flee through the back door. Stretch quickly reads Waldorf his rights. The butler has the right to remain silent and the right to have an attorney present.

But the frightened Waldorf tells all immediately. He puts the finger on two other conspirators, Bronco Blackburne and Jastrow Peevler.

All three are charged with, and later convicted of, conspiracy to kidnap a minor. You have solved your biggest case yet.

THE END

You climb onto your bicycle. Quickly, you ride down along the outside of the fence that encloses the right-field line.

As you near the backstop, you reach down and grab a cracked bat that someone has left leaning against the fence. You round the backstop. As you head down the outside of the fence that runs along the left-field line, you see Big Martin fumbling with the lock on his equipment shed.

Next to him on the ground is the bulging sack. As you pedal closer you can see that something is moving inside it. You know that it is your friend IQ.

You leap off your bicycle while it is still moving, and you draw back the baseball bat.

"Stand back!" you yell at Big Martin, who turns toward you in complete surprise. But he does not move.

You take a vicious swing with the bat that intentionally misses the groundskeeper's stomach by only a few inches. Now he takes a step back.

"Keep going!" you yell as you draw the bat back threateningly.

This time Big Martin turns and runs as best he can.

You lean over and untie the sack. IQ quickly wiggles his way out and takes a deep breath.

"Come on," you say, "get on my bicycle."

Without saying a word, IQ sits on the seat as you swing your leg over and pedal away standing up.

When you are far enough away from the ball field, you call Sergeant Stretch at the Plumtown police headquarters. You tell him the entire story.

"O.K., kid," he says, "we'll handle the whole thing. You take IQ home and make sure he's all right."

"But, Sarge," you say, "I'd still like to work on this one."

"That's O.K., kid, you've done enough. Better let us handle it from here."

THE END

Stretch gets on his police radio and relays what you've told him to the central operator at headquarters, then waits while the information is run through the police computer. He listens to the report and then turns to you and IQ.

"It's Jastrow Peevler at 301 Elm Street," Stretch says, starting the car. "One of the biggest crooks alive. I'm not surprised he's involved in this."

Stretch looks intense as he pulls the car away from the curb. You are not sure who this Peevler character is, but you feel almost sorry for him now. When Stretch gets like this he can be a tough man to deal with.

As you turn onto Elm Street, Stretch slows down and pulls over to the curb about one hundred yards from Peevler's house.

Stretch reaches into the glove compartment and takes out a small pair of binoculars.

"I wonder," he says, holding the binoculars to his eyes, "what our next move should be. Any suggestions?"

If you decide to wait and see what develops, turn to page 111.

If you decide to move in on the house right now, turn to page 107.

104

from page 98

You stay hidden behind the shed. But you peek around the corner and watch Big Martin as he lumbers away.

By the time Big Martin disappears into the baseball league clubhouse, you see Sergeant Stretch pull into the parking lot in his unmarked car.

You run as fast as you can to meet him.

"Hi, kid," he says, slamming the car door behind him.

"They've got Cappy Wiltburrow and IQ," you say quickly.

"Slow down, kid, slow down, one thing at a time," says Stretch.

You explain everything that has happened, including what Big Martin said at the equipment shed.

"Well, let's just get a hold of Martin Broadaxe and find out if that *is* IQ locked in the shed," Stretch says.

Stretch leads the way to the clubhouse. Inside, you find Martin Broadaxe sitting alone having a cup of coffee.

"Broadaxe," Stretch says, holding up his police shield and identification, "I'd like to have a little talk with you."

You watch with amazement as Big Martin's jaw drops and his eyes widen with shock. The cup of coffee slips from his fingers and crashes to the floor.

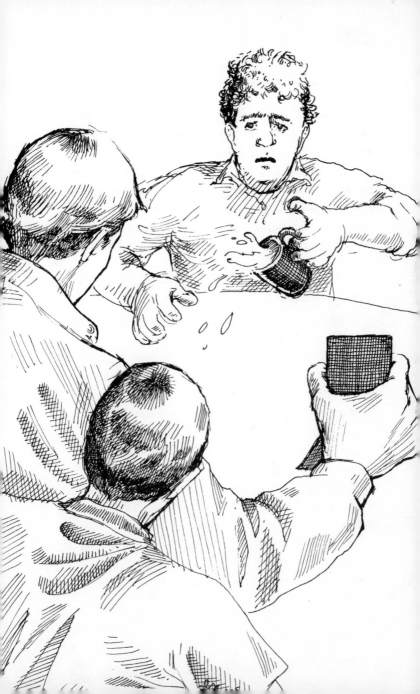

"It's not me," he cries out. "It's not me. They forced me. They forced me. It's those other guys. They're the ones. They forced me into it."

Stretch settles Big Martin down, while you take the key to the equipment shed and run to let IQ out. Within a few minutes, Broadaxe has told everything he knows. Now you know the whole plot, including the location of the kidnapping victim, Cappy Wiltburrow.

THE END

from page 103

"Let's nip this in the bud," you say to Stretch.

"O.K.," he says, "I'll go check the place out. You kids wait here."

You and IQ never like to stay behind, but you always respect Stretch's authority. You watch from the car as he walks down the block and up Jastrow Peevler's driveway.

"What's he doing?" you say.

"Looks like the direct approach," IQ answers, as you both watch Stretch knock on Peevler's front door, his police shield and I.D. out and ready.

No one answers the front door. Stretch strolls around the house toward the back door, out of your view.

Now the waiting begins. You and IQ are both nervous about having lost sight of Sergeant Stretch.

"I'm willing to wait ten minutes, max," IQ says.

"Same here," you say.

IQ monitors his watch closely as you peer through Stretch's binoculars for any sign of movement in Peevler's house. The seconds tick away and Stretch does not reappear.

"Ten minutes!" IQ says suddenly.

"Let's go!"

The two of you bolt from the car and race down the street. As you rush up Peevler's driveway, a gut feeling warns you that what you are doing is extremely dangerous.

You skip the front entrance and head right for the back of the house. When you get there, you find the back door open and you rush inside.

When you realize that it's a trap, it's too late.

"Well, well, well," says Jastrow Peevler with an evil grin. He points a revolver at the two of you.

"Step into the living room," he says. "Your friend is waiting for you. We were just about to sit down for a spot of tea." He laughs viciously and points to the living room with his revolver.

As you and IQ enter the living room, you see Stretch lying face-down on the floor, unconscious, his hands and feet bound. A huge man stands over him.

Peevler orders you and IQ down on the floor and ties up your hands and feet. Then he puts adhesive tape across your mouths.

Peevler and the large man carry you, IQ, and the unconscious Stretch into a closet.

"Have a nice day," Peevler says as he closes the door.

THE END

from page 44

From a pay phone, you call Mrs. Puddington.

"Hello, my brave young friend," she says. "How are you coming on your investigation?"

"Mrs. Puddington," you say, "I have more questions to ask you. May I come out to see you now?"

"Certainly. Come by this very instant," she says.

You say good-by to her and get onto your bicycle. In less than ten minutes of hard pedaling, you are at her front door.

"Come in," she says graciously, leading you into the same room where you and she and IQ sat this morning.

"Now, what questions do you have for me?" she asks.

"You know all there is to know about this town, Mrs. Puddington, including its history," you say.

"Well," she says, "there may have been one detail or another that has escaped me."

"Well, then," you say, "maybe you can tell me who in this town might have a motive for revenge against Cappy Wiltburrow's father, Frederick G. Wiltburrow?"

Mrs. Puddington blinks.

"A motive for revenge against Frederick G. Wiltburrow?" she says, repeating your words.

"Revenge is such a strong word," she says. "I

assure you that I hold nothing against Fred Wilt-burrow. All of that business between us was many, many years ago."

You can see that Mrs. Puddington has lost her cool. You do not say another word.

"Now," she says, "you must go. I can't answer any more of your questions. Go home and stop imagining things."

Mrs. Puddington leads you to the front door and opens it for you. No sooner are you outside than the door slams behind you.

You get onto your bicycle and start to ride away. You turn your head and see that Mrs. Puddington is watching you from a window.

The whole change in her mood happened so quickly. You had no chance to analyze what it all meant. But suddenly you realize that Mrs. Puddington may well be the "powerful interest" behind the plot to kidnap Cappy Wiltburrow.

You double back to Mrs. Puddington's house.

Turn to page 115.

You, Stretch, and IQ wait in the car for something to happen at 301 Elm. A half hour passes. All three of you are becoming edgy.

Suddenly you see Jastrow Peevler's garage door open. Stretch tells you and IQ to slide down in the seat, and he does the same.

The three of you peek over the top of the dashboard. A large black car with dark-tinted windows rolls down the driveway and turns right, away from where your car is parked. The tinted windows prevent you from seeing how many people are inside.

Stretch waits a few seconds and starts the engine. He pulls carefully into the street, giving the black car plenty of room.

"We have a good guess as to where that car is headed," you say.

"To the road on the other side of the woods from the baseball diamond," IQ says.

"That's right," you say.

"Let's hope so," says Stretch. "Otherwise we might be off on a wild-goose chase while Cappy Wiltburrow is taken captive."

"That's doubtful," IQ says. "I think this is the real thing."

Just as you all thought, the black car turns onto the back road where the Wiltburrow limousine picks up Cappy after games.

"I'm betting that they'll park a couple of hundred yards down from where the chauffeur parks the limousine," Stretch says.

"That sounds like a good guess," you say. "So we'll pull over a few hundred yards from where they'll probably park."

"And that would be right about here," IQ observes.

Stretch pulls onto the shoulder of the road and brings the car to a stop. It's time for police headquarters to send backup support. Stretch gets on the police radio.

He makes his request, but the operator at headquarters tells him there are no squad cars available. Every car in service has been sent to the railroad trestle that crosses Campbell Creek at the outskirts of town. There has been an explosion.

"So that's their game," Stretch says.

"They've created a diversion," you say.

"And the ball game should be almost over," says IQ, checking his watch.

"Let's move," Stretch says as he jumps out of the car and walks quickly along the shoulder of the road. You and IQ follow a few yards behind.

You hear wild cheering from the ball field on the other side of the woods.

"That sounds like the end of an exciting game," IQ says.

"It certainly does," you say. "We'd better tell Stretch."

"Hey, Sarge," you call in a loud whisper.

Stretch turns and motions you off to the side behind some large trees. You tell him that the game is probably over.

"Good," he says, and then points through the trees at a spot farther up the road. "There's the Peevler car."

"No one is standing by the car, but it's running. You can bet they've left at least the driver behind," you say.

"Ahem," coughs IQ. "We have about forty-five seconds to act."

"I see two options," you say.

If you decide to take the car first, turn to page 118.

If you decide to take the men waiting in the woods first, turn to page 6.

from page 110

You stash your bicycle behind a brush pile at the edge of Mrs. Puddington's property. Then you circle around behind the house. Making your way from tree to tree, you duck into the back entryway. You open the door and find yourself in the kitchen.

On tiptoes, you go over to the door that leads out of the kitchen. You open the door a crack. Mrs. Puddington is standing at the end of a long hallway. She reaches for a phone that sits on a small table, and then she dials a number.

You let the door close and look around the kitchen. There is a wall phone next to the refrigerator. You carefully lift the receiver from the hook and put it to your ear.

"Jastrow, we're in trouble," you hear Mrs. Puddington say. She has called Jastrow Peevler.

"What do you mean, Priscilla?" Peevler asks.

"That little amateur snoop I warned you about this morning is getting too close to our plan. I want him removed."

"Big Martin has already taken care of his little assistant," Peevler says, "the one they call IQ."

"Well, fine," Mrs. Puddington says. "But I want this one out of the way, too. He's riding his bicycle back into town at this very minute. Now is the time to act."

"Why didn't you say so," Peevler says. "I'll take care of it."

You hear the phone click down on the receiver and then you hear Mrs. Puddington hang up. So that's it, you think. And they even have IQ!

You won't risk a phone call to Stretch from here. But now it will all be simple. You will get back to your bicycle and return to town on the old dirt road that runs along the railroad tracks. That way Jastrow Peevler will never see you.

You will go straight to Sergeant Stretch at police headquarters. Then you will deliver all of your evidence to him. Chances are he'll let you accompany him back to Mrs. Puddington's. Then he will arrest her and Jastrow Peevler, who will probably be at her house trying to figure out how you disappeared from the road back to town.

And Stretch will also send a man to arrest Big Martin Broadaxe, the groundskeeper at the ball field. You hope that Big Martin will confess to having abducted IQ and reveal where your best friend is being held. Then the whole plot will be foiled, and no one will be hurt. You have solved your biggest case yet.

THE END

118

Stretch leads you from tree to tree along the edge of the road until you are only ten yards from the car. Then he signals you to hang back.

Suddenly, like a shot, he charges the black car and yanks open the door on the driver's side. He points his revolver at none other than Waldorf, the Wiltburrow butler. Ordering Waldorf to lie face-down on the seat, Stretch slaps the handcuffs on the frightened butler.

"Come on," he whispers back to you. "Into the car."

You and IQ scramble into the back seat as Stretch pushes Waldorf onto the floor on the passenger's side in front.

"Now," says Stretch, "these tinted windows will work to our advantage. All we have to do is wait for our friends to come to us. It will be a little surprise party."

No sooner have the words left Stretch's mouth when two men—the notorious Jastrow Peevler and Bronco Blackburne—emerge from the woods carrying a bound and gagged Cappy Wiltburrow.

As they approach the car, Stretch pushes down the button to lock the back door. When Peevler reaches for the handle to pull the door open, it doesn't budge.

"Waldorf," shouts Peevler, "unlock the back door."

But there is no answer.

"What the . . .," says Peevler as he yanks the front door.

Stretch kicks the door open, holding his gun straight in front of him.

"Hands up," he says. "Now!"

As Stretch takes care of the two shocked kidnappers, you and IQ untie Cappy Wiltburrow.

"Who won the game?" you ask him.

"We did," Cappy says, "without you there to hit a home run for the Cowboys."

You, Cappy, and IQ all have a good laugh, as Stretch takes Blackburne, Peevler, and Waldorf back down the road to his police car.

THE END

from page 32

You give Stretch and IQ the thumbs-up sign as they enter Nancy's. Then you follow Waldorf at a respectable distance.

As Waldorf takes a left onto Main Street, he begins to walk faster. You cross to the other side of the street and duck into a storefront. You must not let Waldorf see you.

The butler stops at a telephone booth to make a call. You wish that there was some way you could listen to what he is saying, but you can't get close enough without giving yourself away.

Waldorf finishes the call quickly and hangs up the phone. He looks cautiously up and down the street, and then walks off briskly.

You let several seconds go by before you start following him again. Farther down Main Street, Waldorf turns left onto Elm. You walk more quickly now in an effort not to lose him.

Following Waldorf onto Elm, you move up the street rapidly, ducking behind parked cars as you go. Crossing the street and looking around to make sure that he is not being followed, Waldorf walks up the driveway of a rather badly kept house, 301 Elm. You go back to Nancy's to tell Stretch what you've found.

Turn to page 103.